BEFORE ANYONE

had heard of BLACK BEARD,
LONG JOHN SILVER, or
CALICO JACK, there
was a pirate named
~ ROGER ~

TO MARY JANE

Roger, the Jolly Pirate
Copyright © 2004 by Brett Helquist
Printed in Mexico
www.harperchildrens.com
Library of Congress Cataloging-in-Publication Data
Helquist, Brett.
  Roger, the Jolly Pirate / story and illustrations by
Brett Helquist.—1st ed.
    p.   cm.
  Summary: Roger was a lousy pirate because he knew
very little about ships and never struck fear in the heart
of any sailor, until one day when his shipmates were in
grave danger while he was below decks baking a cake.
  ISBN 0-06-623805-6 — ISBN 0-06-623806-4 (lib. bdg.)
  [1. Pirates—Fiction. 2. Humorous stories.] I. Title.
PZ7.H37598Ro 2004
[E]—dc22
                                              2003011431
Typography by Alison Donalty
10 9 8 7 6 5 4 3 2 1
❖ First Edition

ROGER the JOLLY PIRATE

by BRETT HELQUIST

HarperCollinsPublishers

Roger was a lousy pirate. He couldn't tell the starboard from the larboard, the windward from the leeward, or the mizzen from the main.

He smiled instead of scowling, and he grinned instead of growling. He always had a yarn to tell or a sea shanty to sing, and he had never struck fear in any sailor's heart. His shipmates called him Jolly Roger. They didn't mean it nicely.

When there was serious pirating to be done,
the other pirates never wanted Jolly Roger around.
If they planned to board an enemy vessel, make a
prisoner walk the plank, or bury stolen treasure,
they always sent Jolly Roger down to the ship's hold.
This didn't make Roger feel jolly at all.

The pirates on Jolly Roger's ship were the terror
of the high seas. Merchant ships fled at the
sight of them. Sailors surrendered without a fight.
There was only one enemy worthy of their scowls.
He was known as the Admiral.

The Admiral had vowed to bring every
pirate to justice. And at last the day came
when he and his sailors attacked Roger's ship.
Jolly Roger, of course, was sent below.

Up above, the battle began.
Below, Jolly Roger sat wishing he could think of
something—anything—that would make the other
pirates like him.

Then he had a wonderful idea.

He would bake a cake!
In the hold, Jolly Roger spotted something that
looked like a big iron pot.

He happily dumped everything he could
find into the pot and gave it a good stir.

On deck, the cannons boomed and blazed.
The pirates bravely fought the Admiral's men
from port to starboard, from stem to stern.
But the pirates were outnumbered.

As the pirate captain watched the Admiral stride across the deck with his sword held high, he could see that all was lost. He prepared to surrender.

In the dim light of the hold, Jolly Roger found
a wick attached to the pot he had chosen, struck
a match, and sat back to wait for his cake to bake.
He didn't expect what happened next.
Nobody did.

Jolly Roger was blown straight through the
deck and right into the middle of the battle.
He was covered in flour.
He was spotted with soot.
And he was shrieking in terror.

The Admiral's men had never seen anything like it.

"A ghost!" yelped one.

"A skeleton!" screamed another.

The Admiral himself gave the order:

"ABANDON SHIP!"

Jolly Roger was sorry about his cake.
He tried to explain, but no one would listen.
They were too busy cheering.

Jolly Roger still couldn't tell the starboard from
the larboard, the windward from the leeward,
or the mizzen from the main. But his shipmates
didn't care.
In fact, they made a special flag in his honor.
Soon, other pirates began flying the flag. It struck
fear in the hearts of sailors across the seven seas.

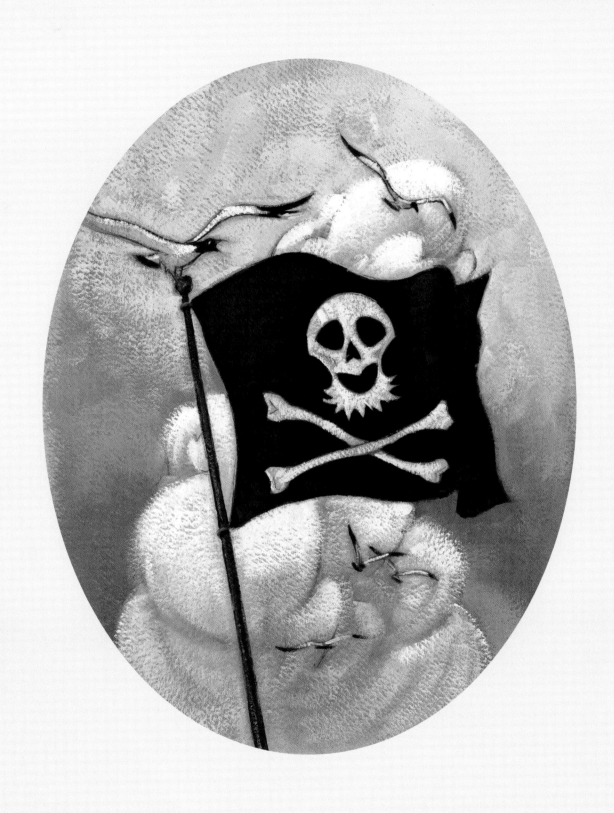

They called it the Jolly Roger.

the Ballad of Jolly Roger

1. What shall we do with our Jol - ly Ro - ger? What shall we do with our Jol - ly Ro - ger?

What shall we do with our Jol - ly Ro - ger? Ear - lye in the morn - ing. 'Way hay, 'n' up she ris - es!

'Way hay, 'n' up she ris - es! 'Way hay 'n' up she ris - es! Dread - ed Jol - ly Ro - ger.

Verses:

2. He always grins while everyone's growling
Always grins when everyone's growling
Always grins when everyone's growling
Earlye in the morning.

3. Put him in the hold till the battle is over
Put him in the hold till the battle is over
Put him in the hold till the battle is over
Earlye in the morning.

4. He made us a cake down in the galley
Made us a cake down in the galley
Made us a cake down in the galley
Earlye in the morning.

5. 'Twas a fine cake till it exploded
'Twas a fine cake till it exploded
'Twas a fine cake till it exploded
Earlye in the morning.

6. Let's make us a flag for Jolly Roger
Make us a flag for Jolly Roger
Make us a flag for Jolly Roger
Earlye in the morning.